Marigold.
with Raffia
Orange
beads

Hyacinth.
Blue
Beads

Violet.
Silk
Flower
Cluster

Petunia.
Paper Taffeta

For Sam

The royalties from this book will go to Birthright,
the medical research charity that cares for the health of mothers and babies.
The Patron of Birthright is HRH The Princess of Wales.
Birthright is the research arm of the Royal College of
Obstetricians and Gynaecologists.
Printed in Scotland by Eagle Colour Books, Glasgow.

THE AMAZING UMBRELLA SHOP was first published in the U.K. in 1990 by
Sidgwick & Jackson, 1 Tavistock Chambers, Bloomsbury Way, London WC1A 2SG.

ISBN 0283 999438

Typeset by Comproom Ltd.

THE AMAZING UMBRELLA SHOP

Story by Shirley Conran
Pictures by Sebastian Conran
Umbrellas by Jasper Conran

In a little white cottage on a small, green hill, lived an umbrella maker. Her name was Miss Annie Adeney. Don't ask me why she had such an odd name, she just did. She'd had it since she was born and everybody spelled it wrongly. She was an orphan, and didn't have a mother or a father. She didn't have any brothers or sisters either. Miss Adeney lived alone with her cat for company. She was often lonely and, because she had spent most of her life by herself, she was very shy, and blushed if anyone spoke to her. But secretly she longed to be popular and get asked to parties.

Miss Adeney made umbrellas in a huge grey factory in the nearby town. There she worked hard all day at her sewing machine, making black umbrellas.

But at night, in her dreams, she made wonderful umbrellas: yellow umbrellas for golfers, spotted blue-and-white umbrellas and great big orange-striped umbrellas. She made pink-and-blue umbrellas for babies' prams, gold umbrellas for pop stars, umbrellas with sewn-on silk flowers for lady gardeners, sunshades with diamond- studded handles for desert sheikhs with lots of oil wells.

In her favourite dream, Miss Adeney saw herself at a Royal Garden Party wearing a pink dress – her favourite colour. Suddenly it started to rain. Immediately Miss Adeney lent her own pink silk umbrella to the Queen, who smiled at her.
But this only happened in her dream and Miss Adeney suspected that dreams never come true.

Miss Adeney lavished all her affection, and what little money she had, on her handsome ginger cat. He had been born in the village at the bottom of the hill. One day, after seeing Miss Adeney buy a kipper from the fish shop, he had followed her home, curled up in front of the fire, and, when Miss Adeney shared her kipper with him, had decided to stay there forever.

The big ginger cat was called Swain, because he had so many admirers among the black, white, grey and brown village cats. He was rather fond of all-night parties, so, after sneaking in at dawn, Swain would sleep all day in front of the fire to get his strength back. He always purred a loud welcome to Miss Adeney when she arrived home from the umbrella factory, and she was very proud of him.

She made him splendid bows for his nightly cat parties, and every evening she tied a fresh one round his neck. Not surprisingly, Swain was a bit vain. He was also rather plump because Miss Adeney liked to prepare special dinners for him.

Every Saturday afternoon, Miss Adeney held a cats' tea-party in the garden. They ate Swain's favourite food – kipper tails and those small silver fish called whitebait.

Every Saturday morning, Miss Adeney cleaned her spotless cottage, before the cats' tea party. Every Sunday morning, she cleared up *after* the cats' tea-party and every Sunday afternoon she worked in her neat little garden.

As if repeating a magic spell, she whispered encouragingly, 'Grow quickly my hyacinths, daffodils, primulas and narcissi.' She was not too shy to talk to her flowers.

But Miss Adeney became thinner and thinner, because she spent so little money on food for herself, and too much on flower seeds and cat food.

Every evening Miss Adeney bicycled back from the umbrella factory. She stopped at the village fish shop, where Swain sometimes met her, and bought supper.

One spring evening, Mr Brigg, the big, friendly fishmonger, lifted his straw boater and said, 'Good evening, Miss Adeney. What shall it be today?' He had a cheerful face and kind eyes. 'I've got a nice piece of turbot', he suggested. 'A beautiful bloater, a pile of silvery sprats, or how about a bit of yellow smoked halibut?'

Miss Adeney, as always, asked regretfully, 'Is that *all* you have, Mr Brigg?'

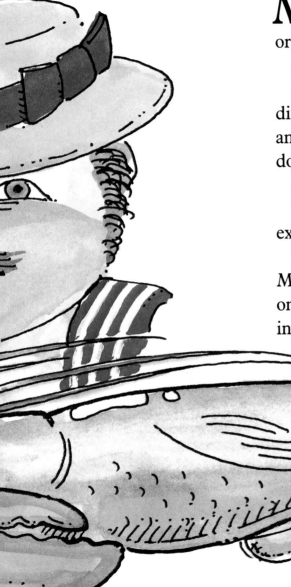

Mr Brigg twirled his moustache and said, 'Can I tempt you with a slithery brown conger eel, or a fresh pink salmon, or cod, or scallops?'

Miss Adeney looked thoughful, then shook her head.

Mr Brigg waved his hand at his white-tiled counter where different fishes were arrayed in beautiful patterns of pink, yellow and white, decorated with parsley. 'We have shrimps, scampi, dogfish, and today – *very* special – some fine cuts of shark.'

Miss Adeney slowly shook her head again.

'How about a plump red lobster?' Mr Brigg suggested. 'A trifle expensive, but worth it, ain't it, Swain?'

The big cat purred loudly at the mention of lobster, but Miss Adeney said, in her firm voice, 'We can only afford lobster on *very* special occasions. What is the tastiest fish in your inexpensive range?'

Mr Brigg said, 'Why, the tastiest fish in our inexpensive range are the kippers. Fresh from Yarmouth this morning, smoked over oak shavings, fit for the Queen herself.'

'That will do nicely,' Miss Adeney said. 'Two fat kippers, if you please, Mr Brigg.'

Mr Brigg carefully picked out two of the plumpest, orange-yellow kippers. He wrapped them up, tied the parcel with a length of green string and handed it to Swain. The cat took it neatly between his little pointed cat's teeth, and carried it home, trotting beside Miss Adeney, as she pushed her bicycle up the hill.

'Swain, did you notice that Mr Brigg had two holes in his socks and a button missing from his shirt front?' Miss Adeney asked.

Of course Swain didn't reply because cats can't talk.

'He spends too much time looking after his shop,' said Miss Adeney. 'That's why he doesn't have time to look after himself.'

M iss Adeney filled the kettle with water for her tea, struck a match, lit the stove and placed the kippers to cook beneath the grill. Then she laid a pink cloth on her kitchen table and set two plates upon it, because Swain always ate at the table. After supper Swain carefully licked his plate with his long, rough tongue until the plate looked as if it hadn't been used.

'Tomorrow is Saturday', said Miss Adeney,' so I shall give the kitchen floor a good polish and then go shopping. I need a packet of poppy seeds for the garden.'

The next morning, Miss Adeney polished the floor until it shone like a skating rink. After shutting all the windows, to keep robbers out, she fetched her pink umbrella and put on her hat and coat. Then she noticed dirty paw marks across the kitchen floor.

'Oh *drat*!' said Miss Adeney, grabbing her mop again and cleaning off the muddy marks. But, as she gave her mop a final twirl, Miss Adeney slipped on the shiny floor and she fell down, CRASH!

SOAP

'Ouch!' said Miss Adeney. 'Bother! Drat and bother!' She tried to stand up, but it wasn't possible. 'Oh dear,' she said to Swain, 'I do believe I have broken my leg.' She started to cry.

Swain didn't know what to do, although he purred very hard and licked the tears away from Miss Adeney's cheeks with his rough, lickety tongue.

'Oh dear,' said Miss Adeney again. 'What *shall* I do?'

Swain rubbed his fat furry body against Miss Adeney's arm, but he couldn't think what to do either.

Miss Adeney cried harder and said, 'Nobody will know I'm hurt. Nobody will come. In the end, we shall starve to death. Oh *dear*.'

MEOW

Swain understood the word *starve*. 'Oh no, not *me*! I must go for help!' he thought, So he ran to the front door on his fat ginger paws, but it was shut. So he ran to each window in turn – but Miss Adeney had carefully closed them.

Swain jumped up the crooked stairs and bounded into Miss Adeney's bedroom, but that window was also shut. He padded into the little bathroom and sprang on to the window ledge. Like the others, this window catch was shut – but it was wobbly. With his damp pink nose, Swain started to push it up. Push, push, push! He pushed until his nose was sore.

Slowly he felt the catch slide up. At last – the window swung open. Swain looked down. Even for a healthy ginger tomcat, it was a very long way to jump to the daffodils in the flowerbed below.

But if Swain didn't jump, then Miss Adeney and Swain would get hungrier and hungrier every day. They would starve to death – shrinking until they were skeletons.

Still Swain didn't jump. It was *such* a long way to the ground.

Suddenly, the ginger cat had an idea. He bounded down the crooked stairs, to where Miss Adeney lay groaning on the floor of the kitchen, her pink umbrella lying beside her.

Swain pounced on the umbrella handle with his sharp, pointed teeth. He dragged the pink umbrella up the crooked, narrow stairs and into the bathroom. Then he jumped on the umbrella spokes to push them up until the umbrella clicked open.

Swain dragged the umbrella on to the window ledge. He looked down at the daffodils so far below.

'It *is* a long jump,' Swain thought. But he didn't want to starve to death, so he shut his eyes, took an enormous breath – and jumped. The ginger cat flew through the air, using the pink umbrella as a parachute.

Swain landed in the flowerbed, crushing the daffodils. Then he dashed down the green hill towards the village.

Mr Brigg, wearing a straw hat and a torn blue-and-white-striped apron, was watering two bay trees that stood in wooden tubs on either side of the door of the fish shop. He had had a busy morning but now all his customers had gone home for their midday meal. 'Dad would be proud of this place,' he said to himself, for his father had worked in the fish shop all his life, and his grandfather before him.

Suddenly, a ginger streak of fur hurled itself at his legs, and he nearly dropped his watering can.

'Gently, gently, Swain,' reproved Mr Brigg, continuing to water the bay trees. Swain was the only cat he liked, because Swain never stole any fish from his shop, unlike the village cats. Fat Swain had quite enough fish without stealing it.

Anxiously, Swain hopped up and down, wishing that he could talk, or that Mr Brigg could understand his purrs and miaows. *How* could he persuade Mr Brigg to go up the hill to help Miss Adeney?

Mr Brigg whistled a tune through his moustache and carefully picked off a couple of dead bay leaves. Swain butted his unpolished shoes, but Mr Brigg took no notice. So, with his sharp, little white teeth, Swain bit Mr Brigg on the ankle.

With a howl of pain, Mr Brigg dropped the watering can and jumped into the air. 'Whatever's got into that dratted cat?' he roared, rubbing his ankle.

Swain took hold of Mr Brigg's dark blue trouser leg and tried to pull him up the street towards the cottage. Mr Brigg yelled, 'Don't tear my trousers, you dratted cat. I've enough in my mending basket as it is'. Angrily, he shooed Swain away from his shop. Swain knew he would have to do something really dramatic. He dodged past Mr Brigg, shot into the fish shop and jumped up on the white-tiled counter. The beautiful pattern of pink, yellow and white fish went slithering in all directions.

Mr Brigg gave a roar of rage and grabbed at Swain, who had leaped across to the expensive lobsters and fastened his teeth around one red claw. But the big ginger cat was too quick for the fishmonger. He flew down from the counter, pulling the red lobster behind him.

Swain ran along the village street, towards the little green hill. Mr Brigg chased after him. His straw hat fell off as he pounded along the road shouting, 'Come back with that, you dratted cat!'

At first Swain ran slowly, so it looked as if Mr Brigg would easily be able to catch him. But whenever Mr Brigg made a grab for him, Swain gave a great leap ahead, to avoid being caught.

Always just ahead of Mr Brigg, the ginger cat ran through the green garden gate, up the path and past the crushed yellow daffodils. He dropped the stolen lobster at Miss Adeney's door.

Puffing along behind, Mr Brigg was out of breath, because he was a plump person and not used to running up hills.

'Cats!' he panted, as he bent down and picked up the red lobster. 'Thieves, the lot of them!' He stood in front of the front door, waiting to get his breath back.

Then he heard a faint voice call, 'Help!'

Mr Brigg looked to the left, but there was nobody in sight. He looked to the right, but he saw nobody.
Again, he heard the voice. 'Help! Help!'

Mr Brigg bent down, pushed up the letterbox and peered through it. He could see the little pink hall leading to the crooked staircase, and the grandfather clock.
Beyond the clock, Mr Brigg could see the shiny kitchen floor . . . upon which lay a pink bundle.

'Miss Adeney, Miss Adeney. Are you hurt?' Mr Brigg called through the letterbox.

'I think I've broken my leg, Who is that?' Miss Adeney called.

'Miss Adeney . . . Annie. . . it's me, Arnold Brigg. This is what comes of living by yourself, with no-one to look after you. I will get help as fast as I can.' Mr Brigg called through the letterbox.

As fast as he could, Mr Brigg ran all the way down the hill, not even stopping to pick up his straw hat. He didn't stop running until he reached the other end of the village and stood, puffing and blowing, at the door of the doctor's house.

By the time it was summer, Miss Adeney had nearly recovered.
One Saturday afternoon she sat in her garden, on a red-striped deckchair, watching Mr Brigg weed her flowerbeds.
Her broken leg, in a white plaster-cast, was propped on a stool
in front of her, and she was darning a big, navy-blue sweater.

Swain lay on the grass beside her. He was wearing an elegant
red collar with tinkling silver bells on it – a present from
Miss Adeney for saving her life.

Mr Brigg stepped back from the geraniums and said,
'Nearly time for supper, my dear. I've brought lobster.'

Mr Brigg called Miss Adeney 'My dear' because they were
going to be married, so that they could look after each other.

Mr Brigg was not tall, dark or dashing, like the heroes in the
romantic novels that Miss Adeney read – but *they* did not exist,
whereas Mr Brigg was *there*. He was very comfortable,
he had a jolly laugh and could make a good cup of tea.

'Lobster! How kind of you, Arnold,' said Miss Adeney.
Instead of eating kippers every evening, they now ate monkfish
on Monday, cod on Tuesday, halibut on Wednesday, trout on
Thursday, salmon on Friday, crab on Saturday and scollops on
Sunday. *Always* with chips. And afterwards they ate ice cream.
Cherry and vanilla ice cream on Monday, green pistachio on
Tuesday, lemon water-ice on Wednesday, tangerine sorbet on
Thursday, toffee-and-walnut ice cream on Friday, chocolate-
chip on Saturday and strawberry whip on Sunday.

As a wedding present, Miss Adeney had made Mr Brigg a splendid gold-handled scarlet umbrella for ceremonial occasions when it rained, which it often does in England.

'My dear, it's good enough for the Queen herself,' Mr Brigg had declared when he first saw it. He often said this about something he liked.

As his wedding present to her, Mr Brigg had offered to buy Miss Adeney her own umbrella shop, next door to his fish shop. Swain could guard the shop at night, to keep out rats and robbers.

Sitting in the deckchair in the garden, and mending the hole in Mr Brigg's sweater, Miss Adeney said, 'I've been thinking, Arnold. I would prefer to have a shop in town. We'll have more customers there.'

'But won't you miss the countryside?' asked Mr Brigg.

'Yes, but I should like a little more excitement,' Miss Adeney told him.

So they moved to London and bought two little shops next door to each other in a street with a famous name – Piccadilly. There they lived, above the shop. Sadly, there wasn't any garden, but Swain was able to meet his new cat friends in Hyde Park at the end of the road, where they could have cat picnics in the summer.

'What colour shall we paint the door of *my* shop?' Miss Adeney asked, thoughtfully.

'Navy blue,' said Mr Brigg in a firm voice. 'That's a fine manly colour, which is why sailors chose it in the first place.' Then, carefully, he added. 'I don't like too much pink around the place.'

'Navy blue it is,' said Miss Adeney.

On the first morning the Umbrella Shop opened, they waited
excitedly – but *not one* customer came in. At lunchtime, a
man came through the door, but he only wanted to know the
way to Hyde Park.

That afternoon, the Queen drove past in her golden carriage,
drawn by six white horses. Her palace was nearby, and you only
had to go to the end of Piccadilly, then turn left, to see it.

When the royal coach passed the Umbrella Shop, they both ran out and cheered, but sadly the Queen was waving to the people on the other side of the street.

'We will put my beautiful scarlet umbrella in the window of our new shop and tomorrow perhaps the Queen will notice it,' said the new Mrs Brigg hopefully.

But the next day, the royal carriage didn't appear.

However, when the scarlet umbrella with the golden handle was placed in the middle of the window, it instantly attracted attention.

First to ring the doorbell was a pretty tight-rope walker with yellow curls. She wanted a white frilly parasol, to help her keep her balance on the rope.

Shortly afterwards two English country gentlemen came in. They wanted umbrella-and-shooting-sticks combined, so that they could watch sheep-dog trials in comfort.

Then came three city gentlemen, in black bowler hats; each one bought a plain black umbrella.

After that came four nuns who also bought plain, black umbrellas.

Five fashionable ladies wanted designer umbrellas to match their dresses, in case it rained at the Races.

And then a dark fat man with very keen eyes came in. He was the most famous photographer in the world, and he wanted six silver umbrellas, to reflect his studio lights.

Next to enter was an elegant, enormous, opera singer from Italy and she said, 'Tra la la, I require seven umbrellas in different colours – one for every day of the week.'

So many customers came into the shop that the navy blue door was never shut until the grandfather clock struck eight.

As Mr Brigg was locking up, his wife said, 'I knew life would be more exciting in town.'

Next morning they were so tired that they could hardly open their eyes. On the doormat lay nine white letters. 'More orders,' beamed Mr Brigg. 'At this rate, my dear, I shall have to give up the fish business and help you.'

That is exactly what happened. Soon Mrs Brigg was machining umbrellas in the most wonderful colours. She used the left-over bits of material to make bow-ties for Swain.

On Monday, Swain now wore a tangerine tie, on Tuesday a brown-spotted one, on Wednesday a purple-striped tie, on Thursday a silver tie, on Friday his tie was green, on Saturday it was scarlet and on Sunday, lemon-yellow silk.

One day a Guards Officer, with a twirly moustache and a very sunburned face, came into the shop. I have travelled far from India,' he said, 'where I used one of your black umbrellas as a sunshade. I was the only chap in the Regiment who didn't get sunstroke. The Maharajah of Pompom would like you to make ten pretty sunshades for his ten little daughters; too much sun gives them a headache which makes them quarrelsome, and the noise is getting on his nerves.'

'What are the princesses like?' Mrs Brigg asked.

The Guards Officer sucked his moustache, thoughtfully.

He said, 'Well, there's Princess Camelia, who's a bit fat, and Princess Petunia, who's a bit thin, and Princess Marigold, who's a bit tall, and Princess Daisy, who is a bit small, and Princess Violet, who bites her nails, and Princess Pansy, who sucks her thumb, and Princess Lobelia, who forgets to wash behind her ears, and Princess Lily, who hates to get up in the morning, and Princess Hyacinth, who won't brush her teeth, and Princess Snowdrop who sometimes . . . wets her knickers.'

'Nobody's perfect,' said Mrs Brigg.

Mrs Brigg made ten silk sunshades, with tinkling silver bells on them (like the bells on Swain's red collar) for the ten little Indian princesses.

M̲r Brigg packed the ten parcels very carefully. Swain licked the stamps, with his rough, pink tongue. 'Why don't they make the sticky part peppermint-flavoured?' he wondered.

Mr Brigg looked at the parcels with pride.
'My dear, we are now in the export business,' he said.
'Lobster for supper, to celebrate.'

Swain was especially happy to be in the export business, because he now had ten more silk bow-ties, all in different colours, made from the left-over bits.

The ten little Indian princesses hardly ever quarrelled again, but twirled their sunshades and smiled, as they listened to the soothing, tinkling silver bells.

After hearing that, Mrs Brigg decided to make some *special* umbrellas – *just* for children.

One morning when Mr Brigg was standing outside the umbrella shop, he looked up at the dark grey sky and said, 'I do believe it's going to rain again, Swain.' He smiled as a drip of rain fell to his nose. 'More customers, ho, ho, ho!'

Happily Swain jumped up and down on the pavement. He knew that more customers mean more lobsters. The more it rained the more umbrellas they sold. People said, 'You can get any umbrella you like at that shop. It's an *amazing* place.'

As Mr Brigg spoke, thunderclouds clapped and the rain fell even more heavily than before. A few minutes later, they both heard horses' hooves clopping in the distance and the faint sound of people cheering.

As the golden coach moved slowly down the street towards them, Swain and Mr Brigg could see that the royal coachmen were soaked to the skin, and the grey horses dripped and shivered as they plodded slowly towards home.

'Perhaps the Queen won't notice us,' Swain worried to himself. 'I shall have to think of something.'

As the golden coach drew close to the Amazing Umbrella Shop, Swain ran inside and jumped up on to the shop window. With his small sharp teeth, he dragged the scarlet umbrella with the golden handle out of the window, out of the shop and into the road, where he danced up and down in the rain holding the umbrella over his head.

JUST WHAT I NEED!

The royal horses stopped. The royal coachmen gazed in amazement. The Queen looked out of the window.

'Why, that clever cat is carrying an umbrella,' said the Queen. 'That's *just* the sort of umbrella that I need for ceremonial occasions.' She looked at the window of the umbrella shop and added, 'I'll also buy that green umbrella, it will be useful for watching polo. And that tartan one would come in handy for the Highland Games.'

Which is why, if you visit the street called Piccadilly, in London, England, you will see above The Amazing Umbrella Shop, a sign which reads . . .

BY APPOINTMENT TO ROYALTY.

Camelia
See Through
Silk

Lobelia
Embroidery
Blue Fringe

Daisy
Felt
Flowers

Snowdrop
Crystal
Drop Beads

Lily
Organza
and leaves.

Pansy
Ve